The Little Red Fort

by
Brenda Maier

pictures by
Sonia Sánchez

Scholastic Press ★ New York

Ruby's mind was always full of ideas.

One day, she found some old boards.
"Who wants to help me build something?"
she asked her brothers.

Oscar Lee pretended not to hear her.
Rodrigo gave her a look that could
melt Popsicles.
José almost fell off the fence.
"You don't know *how* to build anything,"
they said.

Ruby shrugged.
"Then I'll learn."

And
she
did.

"Who wants to help me draw the plans?" Ruby asked.

The boys clutched their sides and howled with laughter.

"Not me," said Oscar Lee.

"I don't think so," said Rodrigo.

"No way," said José. "I'm too busy."

"Fine," said Ruby. "I'll draw them myself."

And
she
did.

Satisfied with her plans, Ruby asked, "Who wants to help me gather the supplies?"

"Not me," said Oscar Lee.
"I don't think so,"
said Rodrigo.
"No way," said José.
"I'm too busy."

"Fine," said Ruby.
"I'll gather them
myself."

And
she
did.

When all the supplies
were gathered, Ruby asked,
"Who wants to help me cut
the boards?"

"Not me," said Oscar Lee.
"I don't think so,"
said Rodrigo.
"No way,"
said José.
"I'm too busy."

"Fine," said Ruby.
"I'll cut them myself."

And
she
did.

When all the boards were neatly cut, Ruby sang, "Who wants to help me hammer in the nails?"

"Not me," said Oscar Lee.

"I don't think so," said Rodrigo.

"No way," said José.

"I'm too busy."

"Fine," said Ruby.
"I'll hammer them myself."

And
she
did.

Soon, Ruby's creation was complete. "Who wants to play in my fort?" she called.

"Me, me!"
said Oscar Lee.
"Let's go!"
said Rodrigo.
"I'll play!"
said José.
"I'm not busy
anymore."

"Not so fast," Ruby said. "You didn't help me draw the plans or gather the supplies or cut the boards or hammer the nails. You said I didn't know how to build.

And you laughed at me.

I'm going to play in the fort by myself."

And
she
did.

"We didn't want to play anyway,"
the boys said.

But
they
did.

So they huddled, whispered, and got straight to work.

Oscar Lee made a mailbox.

Rodrigo planted flowers.

José painted the fort fire-engine red.

Ruby was delighted.

That evening, the boys followed a delicious aroma to a fort-warming party.

"Who wants to help me clean this plate?" Ruby asked.

"We do!"
the boys said.

And
they
did.

BUILD A FORT OF YOUR OWN

KITCHEN-CHAIR FORT

SOFA FORT

BUNK-BED FORT

SNOW FORT

AUTHOR'S NOTE

The Little Red Fort is based on the classic folktale, *The Little Red Hen*. A few years ago, *The Little Red Hen* was the only story my youngest son wanted to hear. About the same time, my other children found some spare boards and lattice, which they used to construct a little fort in the backyard. Both of those ideas swirled together in my mind and became this story.

   The Little Red Hen is a folktale, a story passed down orally. For this reason, it's difficult to tell who first recorded it. Different versions of the story were published in Irish and American magazines and books of short stories as early as the **1860**s. The first version of the story that would seem familiar to you was published in **1874** by a US magazine called *St. Nicholas*. I actually own a copy of the first picture book version of *The Little Red Hen*. It was published in **1918**, so people have been reading it for a century. *The Little Red Fort* pays homage to the classic tale and commemorates its one hundredth anniversary in picture book form!

   I love reading different versions of the story and discovering which parts of the original the author changed. Like snowflakes, no two retellings are just alike! A few of my favorites are: *The Little Red Hen* by Paul Galdone (Clarion Books, **1973**), *The Little Red Hen* by Byron Barton (HarperCollins, **1993**), *The Little Red Hen (Makes a Pizza)* by Philemon Sturges and Amy Walrod (Dutton Children's Books, **1999**), *Mañana, Iguana* by Ann Whitford Paul and Ethan Long (Holiday House, **2004**), and *Little Red Henry* by Linda Urban and Madeline Valentine (Candlewick Press, **2015**). What's your favorite?

Brenda Maier

To my five fort builders: Nicholas, Madison, Katelyn, Christian, and Matthew. — B.M.

To my son, Alex — S.S.

Special thanks to Kira Corngold, Tulsa City County Library researcher, and LeeAnna Weaver, librarian and bookseller,
who ensured I had my facts straight. —Brenda Maier

The art was created using recycled paper, charcoal pencil, pen, gouache, and a combination of traditional and digital
brushes. ★ The text type and display type were set in Sodom Regular. ★ The book was printed on 128 gsm Golden Sun
Matte and bound at RR Donnelley Asia. ★ Production was overseen by Angie Chen. ★ Manufacturing was supervised
by Shannon Rice. ★ The book was art directed and designed by Marijka Kostiw, and edited by Tracy Mack.